THE FERGUSON LIBRARY

3 1118 01107 3718

P9-ELW-770

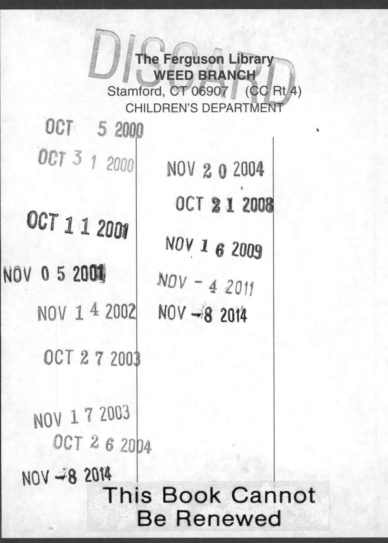

DISCARD

The Ferguson Library
WEED BRANCH
Stamford, CT 06907 (CC Rt 4)
CHILDREN'S DEPARTMENT

OCT   5 2000

OCT 3 1 2000        NOV 2 0 2004

                    OCT 2 1 2008

OCT 1 1 2001

                    NOV 1 6 2009

NOV 0 5 2001        NOV - 4 2011

    NOV 1 4 2002    NOV - 8 2014

    OCT 2 7 2003

    NOV 1 7 2003
      OCT 2 6 2004

NOV - 8 2014

This Book Cannot
Be Renewed

# TRICK OR TREAT COUNTDOWN

by **Patricia Hubbard**

illustrated by
**Michael Letzig**

**Holiday House / New York**

CHILDREN'S DEPARTMENT
THE FERGUSON LIBRARY
STAMFORD, CONNECTICUT

Text copyright © 1999 by Patricia Hubbard
Illustrations copyright © 1999 by Michael Letzig
All rights reserved
Printed in the United States of America
First Edition

Library of Congress Cataloging-in-Publication Data

Hubbard, Patricia.
    Trick or treat countdown/by Patricia Hubbard;
illustrated by Michael Letzig.
        p.    cm.
    Summary:  A counting book that lists scary sights on Halloween,
from one haunted house to twelve creeping cats.
    ISBN 0-8234-1367-5
    [1. Halloween—Fiction.    2. Counting.    3. Stories in rhyme.]
I. Letzig, Michael, ill.    II. Title.
PZ8.3.H8475Tr    1999
[E]—DC21                                                        97-38603
                                                                   CIP
                                                                   AC

In memory of my father—
who taught me to count
—P. H.

For those who count—
Patricia, Michelle, and Steve
—M. L.

**One** haunted house groans.

**Two** tall tombstones moan.

# Three green witches cackle.

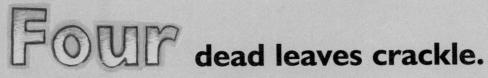 **Four** dead leaves crackle.

Haunted house and witches green,
All make-believe on Halloween.

Five Jack O'Lanterns gleam.

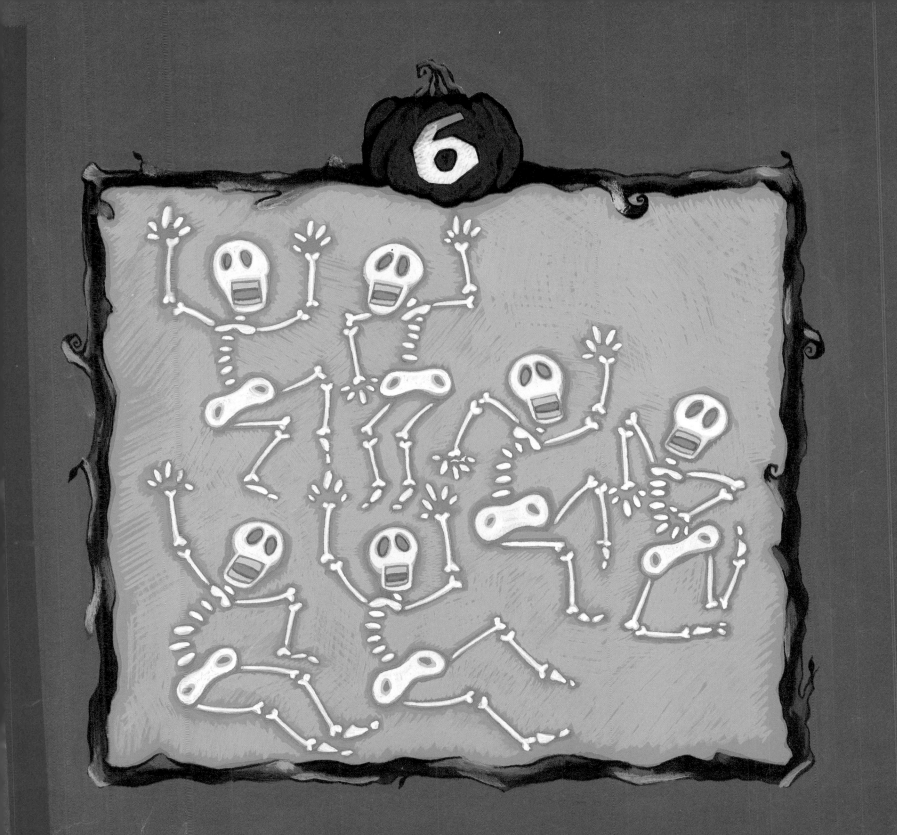

**Six** scary skeletons scream.

**Seven** ghosts whisper, "Oooo."

**Eight** goblins shout, "Boo!"

"Boo"s and "Oooo"s and skeleton screams,

**All make-believe on Halloween.**

# Nine mean monsters prowl.

**Ten** hairy werewolves howl.

**Eleven** black bats glide.

# Twelve creeping cats hide.

Werewolves, bats, and monsters mean,
All make-believe on Halloween.

Twelve hide.

**Eleven glide.**

Ten howl.

Nine prowl.

Eight "Boo"s.

Seven "Oooo"s.

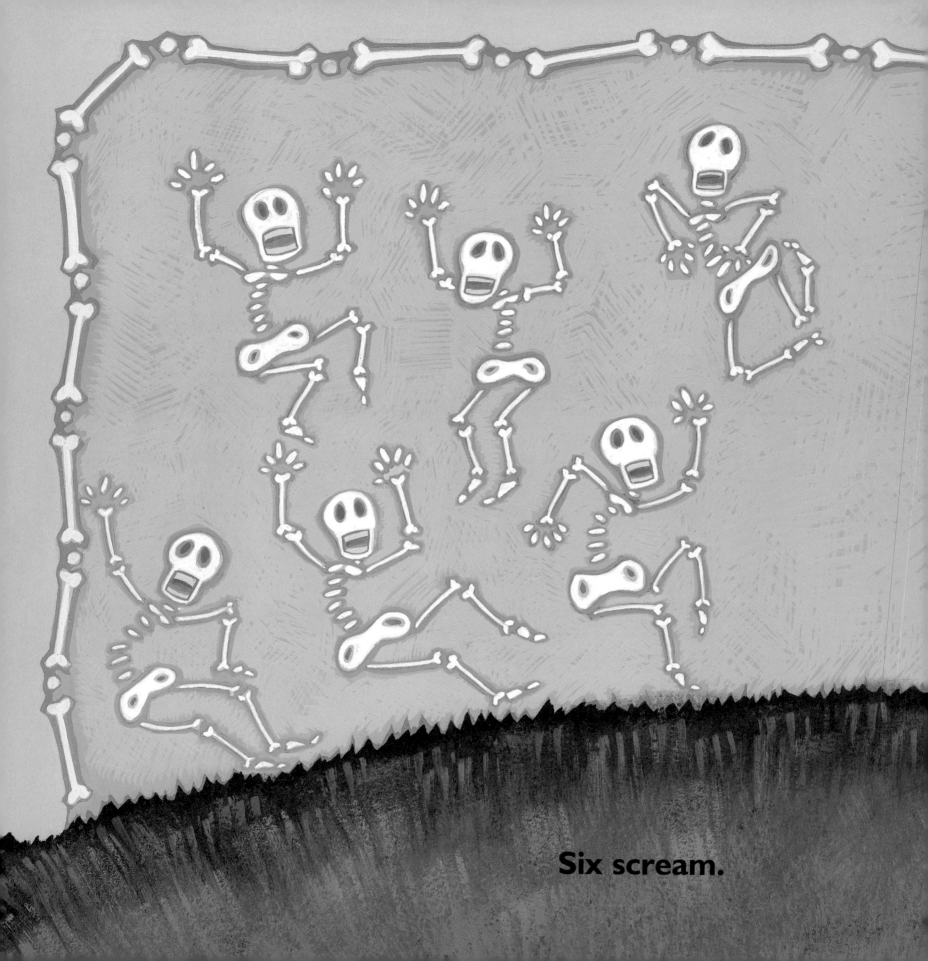

Six scream.

**Five gleam.**

Four crackle.

Three cackle.

A shivery, shivery,
shivery scene,
All make-believe
on Halloween.